Carlotta lives in Germany
Upon her dad's sheep farm.
She tends the little new-born lambs,
And keeps them all from harm.

Wee Jeannie is my Scottish pal.
Her tartan dress looks gay.
She likes to dance the Highland Fling,
When bagpipes start to play.

Angelina comes from Ireland.
The harp she's learned to play.
She says, "There are so many strings,
I practise every day."

Gerda's my Norwegian friend.
She's very fast on skis,
Whizzing down the snowy slopes
Between the Christmas trees!

Now turn to the back of the book.

£2.45

Printed and Published by D. C. Thomson & Co., Ltd.,
Dundee and London.

Dear Girls,
    Here is another great
Twinkle Book specially for you.
    Maria's new shoes, Linda's
lucky penny, Chirpys flying lessons and Rosie Ragdoll
are just some of the super stories you will find inside.
    You'll also enjoy reading about your
favourite "Twinkle" friends — Nurse Nancy, Sam, Benny,
Patch and Elfie.
    There are lots of interesting
puzzles to do, too—and an exciting "Nurse Nancy"
game to play!

    Love from,
        Twinkle

Nancy the little nurse

1 — Nancy and Grandad were busy in the Dollies Hospital. Nancy was going to put a poster on the wall. "It will cheer up the patients," said Grandad.

2 — "I got this poster from my friend, Sarah," explained Nancy. "She brought it back from her holiday in Norway. It shows a view of the snowy mountains."

3 — Later, Nancy gave the dolly patients their elevenses. "These toys are ready to go home for Christmas," smiled Nancy to herself.

4 — Just then, Sarah came rushing into the ward. "Oh, Nancy!" she cried. "Can you mend my skiing dolly, Ingrid? I brought her back from Norway, too." Nancy took the doll to her grandad.

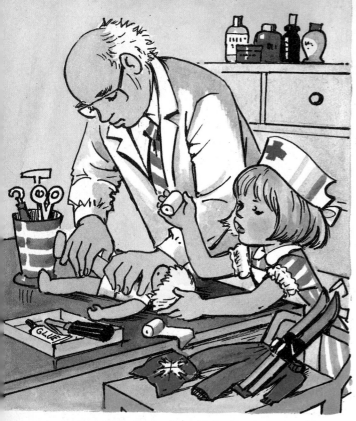

5 — Nancy helped Mr Jingle. "I'm afraid Ingrid will have to stay in hospital over Christmas," sighed Grandad. "Sarah *will* be disappointed," said Nancy.

6 — "Poor Ingrid looks very sad and lonely," sighed Sarah, when she came to visit her doll. "She's the only patient left in the ward. The others have gone home."

7 — Nancy also felt sorry for Ingrid. "I think she must be missing her own country," decided Nancy. "I wish I could cheer her up." As Nancy got ready to go home, she caught sight of the poster from Norway. Suddenly, Nancy had an idea. "I'll ask Mummy if she will help me," said Nancy.

8 — When Nancy got home, she told Mummy about her plan. Mummy agreed to help Nancy. Together, they baked a nice fruit cake. "Now I must ice it," said Nancy.

9 — Nancy's brother, John, helped. When the cake was iced, Nancy decorated it with plastic fir trees. "This cake looks like a little snowy mountain," laughed John.

10 — Nancy was pleased to hear John say that! You see, she hoped the iced cake would make Ingrid feel at home. Nancy took the cake along to the Hospital.

11 — "Look, Ingrid," smiled Sarah, when she saw the cake. "This will remind you of Norway's mountains. I'm sure you'll feel happier now — thanks to Nurse Nancy!"

Maria's new shoes

HANS, the village shoemaker, was getting old. Once, he'd been the finest shoemaker in the land. He'd even made shoes for the king and queen.

Nowadays, though, Hans couldn't see well enough to make fine shoes. He used the wrong colour of thread and his stitching was always crooked. Soon, Hans's customers stopped buying their shoes from him and Hans became very poor.

Mrs Bunn, who owned the baker's shop next door, was Hans's best friend.

"I've brought you some of my tasty chocolate cake, Hans," smiled kind Mrs Bunn, one day.

"Thank you, Mrs Bunn," smiled Hans.

Just then, the royal coach came down the street. Inside were the king and queen and their daughter, Princess Maria. The princess looked very sad.

"Hans, I want you to make a pair of shoes for the princess!" ordered the king.

Poor Hans felt very nervous, as he measured the sad, little princess's foot.

"The shoes must be made of pink satin," added the queen.

When the royal coach had gone, Hans set to work at once.

"Oh, dear!" sighed the old man. "I can't see very well. I hope I can make a pair of dainty shoes fit for the princess."

All day, Hans worked. He was too busy even to talk to Mrs Bunn. So, when a village girl, named Lucy, came to his shop, he didn't even look up.

"Please can you stretch my new red boots, Hans?" asked Lucy. "They're just a little tight for me."

"All right," sighed Hans. "Leave them on the bench. I'll do them later."

Lucy put her boot box down on the bench and left.

All through the night, Hans kept on working on the pink shoes.

"Oh, dear!" he yawned at last. "I'm so sleepy, I can hardly see the stitches I've sewn." And, with that, the old man put his head down on the workbench and fell fast asleep. Hans slept and slept.

Next morning, Mrs Bunn was worried when the old shoemaker didn't come into the shop for his morning rolls.

"I hope he's not ill," said the kind woman. "I'll just close my shop for a few minutes and pop next door to see him."

"Hello, Hans!" called Mrs Bunn. But still old Hans slept on. "Oh, dear!" smiled Mrs Bunn, when she saw her friend still sleeping. "He must be very tired after making the princess's shoes." Then she caught sight of Lucy's boot box.

"The princess's shoes are probably in there," thought the woman. "Hans must have been going to take them to the palace this morning."

Suddenly, Mrs Bunn had an idea.
"I know!" she said. "*I'll* take the shoes to the princess. Poor Hans is too tired to go to the palace today."

So Mrs Bunn set off with the box. She didn't know the princess's shoes were in a drawer in Hans's shop!
Mrs Bunn left the box at the palace. Then she hurried back to tell her friend about her good deed.

However, instead of being pleased with Mrs Bunn, Hans was very cross!
"You silly woman!" he cried. "You've taken the wrong shoes to the princess. Now I will be in terrible trouble!"
Poor Hans waited all day for the angry king to appear at his shop.

Sure enough, later that day, the royal coach drew up outside Hans's shop. Out jumped the princess — wearing Lucy's red boots!

Hans was amazed to see the change in the princess. Instead of being pale and sad, she looked very happy.

"Oh, thank you, Hans!" cried Princess Maria. "These new boots are just what I've always wanted. They're super for splashing around in puddles — much better than silly, pink shoes!" Then the king spoke.

"These boots are perfect, Hans," he said smiling. "They've made the princess very happy. Now we know why she always looked so pale and sad. All she wanted was to go out and play with other children." Then the king gave Hans a big bag of coins and something even better — a new pair of glasses!

"Now I will be able to sew and mend shoes again," smiled Hans. "And it's all thanks to my great friend, Mrs Bunn."

But Mrs Bunn wasn't listening. She was already thinking about baking one of her chocolate cakes for Hans's supper!

Which ballet shoe is the ribbon coming from?

Ballet puzzles

1 2 3

Answer: 2

Can you spot six differences between these two pictures?

Lead Millie through the maze to her dancing class.

You can colour this picture, using your paints or crayons.

The adventures of . . . *Butterfly Brooch*

1 — "I'm bored!" moaned Butterfly Brooch. "Stop complaining!" said Meg Mirror. "Our owner, Pat, is very kind. She washes you and takes you out every day."

2 — "But I want to see the world," sighed Butterfly. "And I want to sleep," grinned Meg. "Be quiet." "Just you wait," said Butterfly. "I've got a plan for tomorrow."

3 — Next morning, Pat put on the brooch and went to the park. As the little girl was feeding the birds, Butterfly tugged at her clasp until, suddenly, it came loose!

4 — The naughty brooch dropped and rolled into the long grass. When Pat went off without noticing she was missing, Butterfly sang for joy. "I'm free!" she cried.

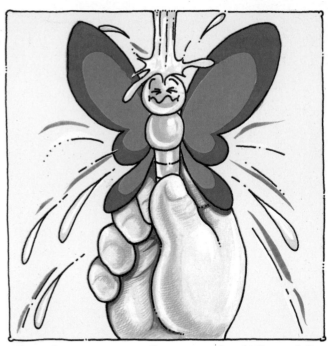

5 — Butterfly was still sitting in the grass when another girl came along. "What a lovely brooch!" she cried. "I'll take you home and give you a wash."

6 — As soon as they reached the girl's house, Butterfly was drenched in cold water. "Brr!" she gasped. "At least Pat used warm water when she washed me."

7 — When she was patting Butterfly dry with a towel, however, the girl let the brooch drop. Down Butterfly fell and landed right on top of a sleeping cat!

8 — "Miaow!" shouted the cat crossly. Then he flicked the little brooch with his paw and sent her flying across the room and out through an open window.

9 — "Help!" wailed Butterfly, as she landed in a flower bed. "I wish I was back home." High above, Jimmy Jackdaw spotted Butterfly's tears glistening in the sun.

10 — The jackdaw loved shiny objects and he snatched Butterfly up in his beak. But the brooch wriggled and jiggled until, at last, the jackdaw let her go again.

11 — This time, when Butterfly fell in a garden, she heard a familiar voice. It was Pat! "My brooch!" she cried. "I'm home to stay," Butterfly told her friends that night. "I'll never say I'm bored again."

Sam

SHONA MACGREGOR has a clever sheepdog called Sam.

They live on a farm in the Scottish Highlands.

One day, Daddy took Shona and Sam on a trip. They were going to visit the Shetland Islands.

"We're going on a ferry boat," Shona told her sheepdog chum.

It was a long journey, but, at last, Daddy pointed to the harbour they were approaching. There was a market at the quay side. Shona loved the thick, woolly jumpers on sale.

"They *are* nice," agreed Daddy. "But they're too dear. I can't afford to buy you one."

2 — The visitors were just leaving the market stall, when there was a loud roar behind them. It was a young couple in a sports car.

"They're going too fast!" gasped Shona.

Later, Shona and Daddy hired bicycles. They cycled out into the countryside.

Suddenly, Daddy pointed down a lane. There were some Shetland ponies on the road.

"They are wild ponies," explained Daddy. "They roam around the islands."

3 — Suddenly, Sam began to growl. The sheepdog had heard something in the distance.

"What is it, Sam?" asked Shona. Just then, Shona and Daddy heard the noise, too.

"Oh, no!" cried Shona. "It sounds like that young couple in their sports car again! I hope they're not driving so fast now."

4 — "We must warn the couple that there are ponies on the road!" gasped Daddy. While he and Shona got ready to wave down the car, Sam knew he had to act fast, too.

Using his sheepdog skills, the clever dog began to round up the ponies and quickly drive them down the lane, away from the approaching car.

"Well done, Sam!" called Shona, when she saw what her pet was doing. Soon the ponies were safely off the road. Sam made his way back up the lane.

5 — The sheepdog was just hurrying back to Shona, when the sports car, which was trying to slow down, threw up a stone. It caught Sam on the side of his head.

The poor sheepdog was dazed, as he lay on the ground.

At first, Shona didn't realise anything had happened to Sam. Then she saw him lying by the side of the road.

"Look, Daddy!" cried Shona. "Sam has been injured." The two MacGregors raced down the lane. But they were surprised to see someone at Sam's side, before they reached him!

6 — It was the Shetland ponies. Two of them had rushed over to Sam and were gently licking the sheepdog's head.

Soon Sam was able to sit up. After a rest, he seemed much better.

"I think Sam will be all right now," said Daddy.

Slowly the MacGregors cycled off down the lane with Sam.

"At least the ponies were safely out of the car's way," said Shona.

"Yes," said Daddy. "I wonder where the couple were going in such a hurry?"

7 — Much farther down the lane, the MacGregors caught sight of the sports car again! It was lying in a ditch.

"Perhaps we can help to move it," said Daddy

Suddenly, Shona had an idea. She told Sam to go back down the lane.

"Where is Sam going?" asked Daddy.

"I think we may need extra help to move that car," said Shona.

8 — The driver explained he was a vet on his way to an urgent call. Mr MacGregor tried to help him move the car, but it wouldn't budge.

Meanwhile, Sam had been busy, too. Shona had told her clever chum to go and round up some of his Shetland pony friends. The sheepdog soon did this.

Then the vet made some harnesses from rope. He put them over the ponies' heads and shoulders. Slowly, the ponies began to pull the car out of the ditch.

9 —"Thanks to Sam and his pony chums, I can now go and see to my animal patients," smiled the vet. "But I won't drive so fast."

All too soon, the MacGregors' short holiday was over.

However, before they boarded the ferry, the young couple they'd helped came to see them off. They had a present for Shona. It was one of the lovely, woolly jumpers Shona had wanted!

"What an exciting visit this has been, Sam," smiled Shona, as the ferry set sail for home.

Little Kitty

I SAT down to knit
  With my needles and wool,
When, all of a sudden,
  I felt a sharp pull.

Crouched down by my feet
  Sat that mischievous Kitty.
She tugged at my knitting,
  So soft and so pretty.

She clambered and climbed
  Up to where I was sitting,
And wrapped herself up
  In my beautiful knitting.

It's plain as can be,
  I just can't knit today,
For mischievous Kitty's
  Decided to play!

Linda's lucky penny

1 — Linda was playing in the garden. She felt very sad. Since her daddy had changed his job, Linda and her parents had moved to a new house in another town.

2 — "I miss my friends," sighed Linda. don't know anyone here." "What a cross face!" said a voice. It was Linda's next-door neighbour, Mrs Butler. Linda liked her.

3 — Mrs Butler had something for Linda. "It's a new penny," she said. "It will bring you luck." Mummy found a red leather purse for the penny.

4 — "Perhaps my lucky penny will bring me friends," smiled Linda. She went out into the garden. Linda heard children's voices. "Would you like to play with my ball?" she called.

5 — But the children were having too much fun to hear Linda. "I don't like living here," sighed Linda to herself. "No one wants to be my friend."

6 — Just then, Daddy came home. He had a present for Linda. It was a cute, little puppy. "Oh, Daddy, she's lovely!" cried Linda. "I wonder what I'll call her?"

7 — When Linda went outside, the other children hurried over to see her puppy. "Now I'll make lots of new friends," thought Linda happily. "I think I'll call my puppy Lucky. Mrs Butler's penny certainly brought *me* luck today."

The *fairy dancer*

JACQUELINE and her mummy were decorating the Christmas tree on Christmas Eve.

"Look, here's the fairy!" cried Jacqueline. "Isn't it lovely to see her again!"

"Yes," Mummy agreed.

"She's just like a ballerina," sighed Jacqueline. "I do hope *I* can be a ballerina some day."

That night, Jacqueline couldn't sleep, so she went downstairs to fetch a drink of water.

As she passed the Christmas tree, she heard someone calling her name. "Hello, Jacqueline! It's me, Serena, the Christmas Tree Fairy."

"I know you want to become a ballerina, Jacqueline. So, if you like, I'll take you to the Fairy's Ballet School," grinned Serena. "Come along. You'll be back in time for Christmas Day."

Serena waved her magic wand and, suddenly, Jacqueline was surrounded by glittering stars. She began to feel herself growing smaller and smaller, until soon she was the same size as Serena.

Then Jacqueline found herself in a garden. The sun was shining warmly and the flowers were all in bloom. There was no sign of any snow.

"This is the Fairy's Ballet School and this is your teacher, Madame Lena," said Serena.

Madame Lena looked carefully at Jacqueline.

"Well you can't dance in that nightgown," she said. Serena waved her magic wand again and, in a flash, Jacqueline was wearing a beautiful white tutu and pink satin ballet shoes.

Now she noticed a door in the trunk of the apple tree. Madame Lena led her through, into the training room. The walls were covered in mirrors and had barres for dance practice fixed to them. Other fairies were practising their steps.

Madame Lena clapped her hands. "Class will begin!" she said.

Excitedly, Jacqueline took her place in the class.

The first thing Jacqueline learned was the five feet positions.

"Now, like this!" called Madame Lena. "One, two, three. Stand up straight. Tummy in. Chest out. Very good."

Jacqueline tried very hard and Madame Lena was pleased with her.

"You could be a wonderful ballerina. Remember, you must be as graceful as a gazelle, as light as a butterfly and *smile*! Show everyone how you are enjoying yourself," she told Jacqueline.

All too soon it was time to go. Serena waved her wand and Jacqueline found herself back in her home, beside the Christmas tree.

"Thank you, Serena," she whispered. "I've had a lovely time."

But Serena said nothing and Jacqueline wondered if it had all been her imagination. However, when she returned to her room she saw the white tutu and the tiny satin ballet shoes on her pillow and knew it had been real.

The next day was Christmas Day. Excitedly, Jacqueline opened her presents and found a beautiful pair of real life-size ballet shoes.

"Are they for me?" she gasped.

"Certainly," said Mummy. "And we've enrolled you in a dancing school. You start next week."

"Unless you've changed your mind about dancing," chuckled Daddy.

"Of course not. Watch me!" cried Jacqueline. Hurriedly she put on the shoes and showed her parents what she had learned in the Fairy's Ballet School.

"That's *very* good," gasped Mummy. "When did you learn that?"

Jacqueline winked at the fairy on the Christmas tree.

"That's a fairy secret," she laughed.

Benny's Holiday

WE all stayed at a farmhouse for
  Our holiday this year.
When we arrived, a real cream tea
  Was waiting for us here.

Next morning, we woke up at dawn.
  The sun rose in the sky.
"A-cock-a-doodle-do!" we heard
  The barnyard cockerel cry.

Down in the meadow, by a stream,
  A dear old donkey stood.
"Oh, may I have a ride?" begged Ben.
  The farmer said he could.

Sometimes, up in the stable loft,
  We used to go and play,
And once we found sweet kittens there,
  Curled in a nest of hay.

The farmer took us both to see
A lovely, newborn calf.
It was so wobbly on its legs,
It made young Benny laugh!

One day, we visited the pigs,
A-grunting in their pen.
Proud Mrs Porky had some babes—
We counted eight, nine, *ten*!

On our last day, we went to see
The cows milked, side by side.
"I *love* the one called Buttercup!"
My funny brother cried.

We felt so sad to say good—bye.
"Cheer up!" the farmer said.
"Here are wee kittens for you both!"
That made us smile, instead!

Here's a chance to help Nurse Nancy in the Dollies Hospital and play a super fun game! All you need is a dice and the counters on the right. Cut these out, paste them on cardboard and give one to each player. Throw a six to start, then, next throw, off you go.

The first player to reach the finish is the winner.

20

21

22
Miss a turn while you join Nancy at Dollies Hospital tea party.

23

24

19

25
Deliver a repaired teddy. Go forward 2 places.

18

26

27

You're soaked bathing a doll. Go back 4 places to change.

17

28
Run back to 18 to fetch doll after dog runs away with it.

16

14

15

29

Finish

Chirpy's flying lessons

CHIRPY CHICK popped out of her eggshell, one sunny morning, and looked all around her. She watched the daffodils blowing in the breeze. Then she spotted Lucy Lark rising from her nest. As Lucy flew high up in the sky, Chirpy wished she could follow her.

"I don't want to live in a chicken pen," she told her mummy. "I want to live in a field and fly in the air like Lucy."

"But chickens don't fly like larks," laughed Mummy. "You *are* silly Chirpy." However, Chirpy wouldn't listen.

"I'm sure *I* could fly," thought Chirpy, as she hurried off to find Lucy.

"Can you teach me to fly?" Chirpy asked Lucy.

"Well, I've never seen a chicken fly before," said Lucy, "but I suppose I could give you some lessons."

"First, flap your wings," began Lucy. Chirpy did that. Then she ran along the ground, still flapping her little, yellow wings.

"Try to fly now!" called Lucy. Chirpy jumped up and down, but, instead of flying through the air, the little chicken landed with a bump on the ground!

"Never mind," said Lucy. "Let's try again." But it was no use. Chirpy couldn't get off the ground.

"I'm afraid I can't teach you," sighed Lucy, as she flew away.

But Chirpy was determined not to give up.

"I know what I'll do," she thought. "If I climb on to a rock and jump off it, perhaps that will help."

Just then, Susie Starling and Stan Sparrow came along.

"What's that silly chicken trying to do?" asked Stan.

"I'm trying to fly," said Chirpy, who'd heard the cheeky sparrow.

"But chickens don't fly," laughed Susie.

By now, another bird had come along to look at Chirpy. It was Percy Plover.

"I can take you flying, Chirpy," he said kindly. "Climb on to my back."

"Whee!" cried Chirpy, as she and Percy soared through the air. "This is nearly as good as flying by myself."

But Chirpy was enjoying herself so much, she forgot to hold on tightly. The next thing she knew, she found herself floating through the air — without Percy!

"Help!" she cried. Luckily, the little chicken landed on some soft ground.

"I think flying is really too dangerous for a chick," decided Chirpy. Then she felt some spots of rain.

"Oh, no!" she cried. "I'm going to get wet. I must find somewhere to shelter."

Chirpy knew she was a long way from home. As she hurried along the fields, she caught sight of Lucy Lark.

"Hello, Lucy!" called Chirpy. "Can I shelter in your nest?"

"I'm afraid there isn't enough room for you," said Lucy. "You should hurry home to your own house."

And that's just what Chirpy did. Her mummy *was* pleased to see her.

"Well, how did your flying lessons go?" asked Mummy, as she cuddled her wet, little chick under her cosy wing.

"Mm," said Chirpy, yawning. "Learning to fly is tiring. I don't think I'd like to be a lark after all. It's much better being a chick, and living in a nice, warm chicken house!"

Dotty Doodles

She's quick on the draw with felt-tip pens.

1 — Hello, readers. I've drawn a girl. She's called Alice.

2 — Alice loves flowers, so I'll draw some just for her.

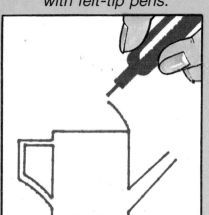

3 — But flowers need water. I'll draw a watering-can.

4 — Alice waters the flowers with her new watering-can.

5 — Phew! It's hard work for Alice. But I've an idea.

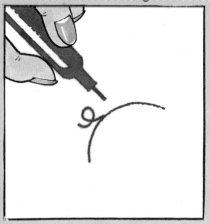

6 — I'll draw someone to help Alice. It's an elephant.

7 — Little Elsa Elephant fills her trunk with water . . .

8 — . . . and begins to water the flowers! Alice *is* pleased.

Elfie

Elfie is a tiny elf who lives secretly in Mary's doll's house. When he makes things happen, Mary thinks it is magic. Poochie, Mary's big dog, is Elfie's best friend.

1 — Elfie had been invited to a fancy dress party. He looked out all his costumes. "I wish I had something unusual to wear," he sighed. "I've worn everything before."

2 — That afternoon, Elfie watched Mary making Christmas cards for her family and friends. "They look pretty with glitter on them," Elfie thought.

3 — Suddenly, the little elf remembered he had to get ready for the fancy dress party. He dashed across the floor and slipped on some spilled glue. "Oh, no!" wailed the elf. "I can't stop!"

4 — Elfie tried to keep his balance, but it was no use. He fell down and was covered with the glue. "I'll have to take another bath!" he said, crossly. "And I haven't much time!"

5 — Just then, Mary knocked some glitter off the table. If floated down and stuck to the glue on Elfie's clothes. "This is awful!" Elfie cried, and stamped his foot.

6 — "I'm going to be late for the party now," thought Elfie. "It will take me *ages* to wash off all this glue and glitter!" The little elf hurried across the playroom floor and into Mary's doll's house.

7 — But, when Elfie saw himself in the mirror, he stopped being cross. "I won't need to change after all," he said with a laugh. "I *am* glad."

8 — At the party, Elfie's friends gathered round to admire his costume. "What *are* you?" they asked. "I'm a Christmas tree decoration!" replied Elfie with a grin.

Mari's magic wand

MARI was one of the merriest witches in Toadstool Village — except when it was time to go to school!

You see, something always seemed to go wrong with Mari's spells.

If the lesson was to magic brown rabbits white, Mari's were sure to turn out pink. Or if the little witches were asked to fly, poor Mari would always fall to the ground.

"Come on, Mari!" called Witch Wanda. "Stop daydreaming or you'll be late again."

Mari was always last in school, so, every day, she was left with the oldest, most battered magic wand to use.

The first lesson of the day was to magic up a beautiful gown. All the little witches practised with their magic wands.

Witch Zenda was first. She waved her wand, chanted a spell and suddenly a lovely gown appeared in a flash!
The other witches were impressed.

"Do you like my gown, Mari?" Zenda grinned.
"Er — it's quite nice," said Mari, bravely. "But mine will be even nicer!"

Wizard Wizzy, the teacher, and all the other witches gathered round as Mari waved her wand and sang a spell.
Fizzle! Crack! There was a sudden flash! But, instead of a beautiful gown, a raggedy old dress appeared!

"Oh, dear!" gasped Mari. "I seem to have done something wrong again."
"Nothing out of ten again, I'm afraid, Mari," sighed Wizard Wizzy.

Poor Mari was terribly upset. She cried all the way home. Between her sobs, she explained to her mother what had happened.
Mari's mother couldn't understand what was wrong with Mari's spells until she saw the battered old wand that Mari had brought home.

"Is this the wand you used at school?" asked Mari's mother.
"Yes," grumbled Mari. "I *always* end up with that one."
"This wand has a crack in it," said Mari's mother. "And that's sure to mix up spells. Wait a moment."

Mari's mother went to a cupboard and pulled out an old box. From inside the box, she lifted a shiny black wand with a gold star on top.

"This was your grandmother's wand," she told Mari. "Use it tomorrow, and I'm sure your spells will turn out right."

The next day, Mari was so excited that she could hardly wait to get to school.

At last, it was time for spell practice.

One by one, the little witches magicked an apple into a crown. Then it was Mari's turn.

Everyone gasped when Mari made the most beautiful crown of all appear!

Wizard Wizzy was delighted!

Even Witch Wanda and Witch Zenda had to grin, especially when Mari magicked up two super cakes for a celebration party.

"I'm a proper witch at last!" Mari cried happily.

Santa's puzzle-time

Unscramble the letters to find to which countries the sacks are going.

Lead Sammy through the maze to his fort.

Answers: CHINA, ITALY, FRANCE, BRITAIN.

Try to spot six differences between these two pictures.

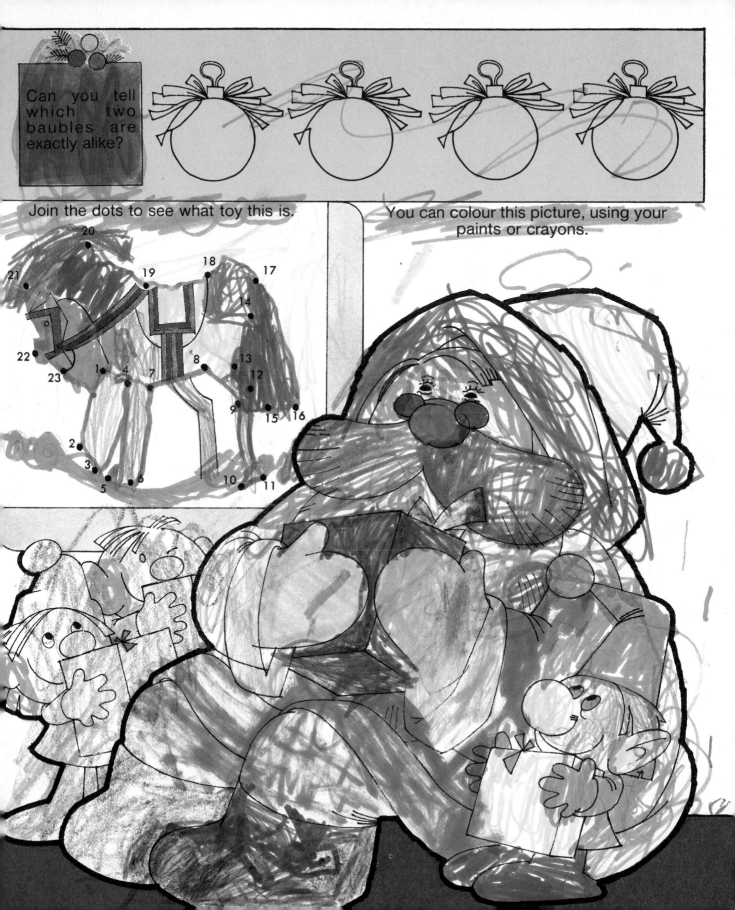

Can you tell which two baubles are exactly alike?

Join the dots to see what toy this is.

You can colour this picture, using your paints or crayons.

My favourite dolls

I'VE got a lot of pretty dolls.
   My fairy doll is Fay.
She has a wand and silver wings,
And points her toe all day.

My baby doll looks, oh, so real!
Her name is Natalie.
Mum lets me wrap her in the shawl
I had, when I was wee.

Anita is a doll from Spain.
She has a painted face,
And wears a black mantilla, with
A dress of pretty lace.

My walking-talking doll is fun.
She nods and says, "I'm Jane!"
I feel so very proud of her,
When we stroll down the lane!

Dear Rosie is my old rag doll,
She isn't big or small.
Her face is worn, her frock is torn —
I love her best of all!

Jenny goes to sea

JENNY ONE was a small fishing boat who belonged to Skipper Joe. Together, they caught lobsters in the bay. It was a nice, easy life, but Jenny wasn't very happy.

"I want to go far out to sea like you," she told the big fishing boats.

The big fishing boats laughed when they heard her. "You're much too small," they chuckled. "The waves would swamp you and you'd sink!"

One morning, Skipper Joe ran down to the harbour, looking worried.

"There's been a storm warning," he told Jenny. "We'll have to hurry and collect all the lobster pots."

Skipper Joe started Jenny's engine and the little boat chugged out of the harbour.

They soon collected all Skipper Joe's lobster pots from the bay.

"Now we can go home," smiled Skipper Joe and headed Jenny back to the harbour. However, Jenny wasn't feeling well.

"My engine feels all funny," she thought.

Just then, Jenny's engine spluttered and stopped.

"Oh, my goodness!" gasped Skipper Joe. "What can be wrong? You were all right this morning."

Skipper Joe looked at Jenny's engine.

"Oh, dear!" he sighed. "I'll have to call the lifeboat to tow us home, or we'll be carried out to sea."

"Out to sea!" thought Jenny. "Hooray!" Jenny suddenly felt herself being pulled along by strong currents.

"This is fun!" she laughed. But the little boat began to change her mind as the sea grew rougher and rougher.

Skipper Joe radioed the lifeboat. By this time, the waves were quite high. Some of the bigger ones broke over Jenny. Jenny felt the water trickling inside her.

"I don't want to sink," she sobbed.

Just as Jenny One had given up all hope of ever being rescued, however, Skipper Joe gave a shout.

"The lifeboat!" he cried. "We're saved!"

The lifeboat crew quickly tied a line on to Jenny One and began towing her towards the harbour. Soon, the water became calmer and the waves smaller. Jenny One breathed a sigh of relief.

"Hooray!" the big boats cheered when Jenny went into the harbour. "We were worried about you."

"Thank you," said Jenny, shyly.

Later that evening, as Jenny One rocked quietly at her moorings, she thought about her adventure.

"I'm glad I don't have to go beyond the bay," she decided. The big boats were right to laugh at me wanting to go to sea. It's much too wild and scary for me!"

With that, the little boat drifted off to sleep, dreaming about lobster pots in a nice, calm bay.

Twinkle's

*E*IGHT-O-CLOCK . . . the morning sun
    Shines brightly on my bed.
Time for breakfast. Time to dress.
    A busy day ahead.

Nine-o-clock . . . and time for school.
    I am nearly ready.
With my lunch box and some pens,
    And my furry teddy.

Eleven-o-clock . . . there's the bell.
    It's time to play a while.
We skip and shout and chatter,
    And chase and jump and smile.

One-o-clock . . . my rumbling tum
    Is ready for some lunch,
I've cheese and rolls and apples,
    A lovely lunch to munch!

day

Four-o-clock . . . and school is through.
  I'd better change my dress.
Then I'll ride my bicycle,
  And call for Jane and Tess.

Five-o-clock . . . and time for tea.
  There's a nice cooking smell.
Mummy says that Jane and Tess
  Can stay for tea as well.

Seven-o-clock . . . I've had my bath.
  I'm pink and scrubbed quite clean.
Can't stop yawning. Clean my teeth.
  What a day it's been!

Eight-o-clock . . . and lovely dreams,
  As off to sleep I fall.
Good! Tomorrow's Saturday,
  My favourite day of all!

Teddies' picnic puzzles

You can colour this picture, using your paints or crayons.

Try to spot six differences between these two cakes.

Can you tell which two flasks are exactly alike?

Lead Teddy through the maze to the picnic.

Silly Ronny Reindeer

RONNY the reindeer was always getting into trouble. He wasn't very clever and looked so funny, that the other reindeer laughed whenever they saw him.

One morning, Ronny arrived for sleigh practice wearing wellies and a scarf.

"Why are you dressed like that?" gasped Santa.

"It's cold," replied Ronny.

"You look silly!" snorted Santa.

All the reindeer took their places in front of the sleigh and started to pull. But, oh, dear! Ronny's scarf began to unwind and tangle up the reindeer team! Santa *was* cross.

"Your scarf has ruined the practice, Ronny," he scolded. "We'll meet again at midnight ,everyone. And, Ronny, remember no silly scarf or wellies at *that* practice, please."

The midnight practice started without a hitch. Ronny and the other reindeer took off into the sky very smoothly.

"Well done!" called Santa. "Now, we'll practise landing on a roof."

The reindeer team managed this easily, too. Ronny was beginning to feel very pleased with himself. So pleased, that he began to grow careless.

"Watch out!" cried Santa.
But it was too late. Ronny galloped straight into a village Christmas tree, pulling the sleigh, Santa and his reindeer chums with him!

"I'm sorry," mumbled Ronny and hung his head in shame. "I don't know why I'm so silly. I'll be more careful next time."

"There won't be a next time," said Santa, sternly. "It's Christmas Eve and the next run isn't a practice. I can't risk any accidents with children's presents aboard."

Once Santa had loaded the sleigh, he set off with the other reindeer. Ronny *was* sad.

"I'm useless!" he sobbed.

Suddenly, Ronny noticed a sack of presents on the ground.

"Oh, no!" gasped Ronny. "One of the sacks of presents has been left behind!"

Ronny grasped the sack between his teeth and set off after Santa. At last, he caught up.

"Ronny!" Santa cried, when he saw the reindeer. "What are you doing here?"

Ronny dropped the sack into the sleigh.

"You left this behind," he gasped.

"Thank you, Ronny," said Santa, gratefully. "A lot of children would have been disappointed if you hadn't brought that sack!"

As a special treat, Santa let the clever reindeer ride in the sleigh. Ronny *was* pleased.

"I'm not such a useless reindeer after all," he thought, with a smile.

Patch

1 — Paula Perkins has a kitten called Patch. He likes to join in with everything Paula does. Paula's friend, Beth, had come to visit. "Let's play skittles," said Paula.

2 — Patch wanted to play, too. However, he kept knocking down the skittles when it was Beth's turn. "Oh, Patch!" sighed Paula. "You're ruining our game."

3 — Next, the girls played snakes and ladders. But Patch wanted to play with the dice. "Let's go into the garden," said Paula. "Patch can stay indoors."

4 — Paula fetched two bats and a ball. "Patch can't play *this* game," grinned Paula. Then Beth hit the ball too hard. It became stuck in the branches of a tree.

5 — Patch hurried out of the house. The clever, little kitten knew he could help Paula and Beth. He climbed up the tree and pushed the ball out of the branches!

6 — "Well done, Patch!" smiled Paula. "You can join in our game after all. You'll be our ball-boy." "You mean our *ball-kitten*!" giggled Beth. And little Patch purred loudly, as if to agree!

Paper-plate people

To make one of these super puppets, you will need 2 paper plates, a piece of thin card, 10 cm x 7 cm, glue, paints or crayons, a piece of material and a rubber band.

1. Glue the plates together, like this, leaving 5 cm unglued at the bottom.

Next, roll the thin card into a tube, push it into the 5 cm gap between the plates and glue it in position.

2.

3.

Now you can paint on the puppet's face and hair. Or, if you like, you can stick on wool for hair and add ears and noses made from card.

To dress the puppet, gather the piece of material round the neck and secure with the rubber band. Cut holes where your thumb and pinky are, to make the puppet's arms.

Rosie Ragdoll

1 — Rosie Ragdoll got out of bed one sunny, spring morning and decided to have a tea-party for her friends. "But, first, I must tidy up my house," said Rosie.

2 — After she'd had breakfast, Rosie fetched a duster and began to dust. Soon, her bedroom looked neat. "Now I'll start on the sitting-room," thought Rosie.

3 — Rosie worked all morning. In the afternoon, she went into the village. At the post office, Bobby Badger had a parcel for Rosie. "It's from your granny," said Bobby.

4 — Rosie opened the parcel when she got home. Inside was an egg. "I'd better keep this egg warm, so that it will hatch," thought Rosie.

5 — Then Rosie sat on her rocking-chair and dreamed about her egg. "When the egg hatches, I'll have a nice, brown hen to lay more eggs for me," smiled Rosie.

6 — Next day, was Rosie's tea-party. Rosie poured out the tea. "This tea is cold!" complained Teddy. "Why don't you use the tea-cosy to keep your tea-pot warm?"

7 — "I'm using my tea-cosy to keep my *egg* warm," explained Rosie. Teddy looked at the egg. "But it's a *chocolate* egg!" he laughed. "And now it's all melted."

8 — Poor Rosie *was* upset. "I thought it was a real egg," she sobbed. "Never mind," said the toys kindly. "We'll soon clean up the melted chocolate."

9 — The toys didn't take long to clear away the chocolate egg. But Rosie still looked miserable. Suddenly, Teddy had an idea. He whispered it to the others.

10 — Next day, the toys called round to see Rosie. They brought her a present. It was another chocolate egg. "I won't try to hatch this one!" said Rosie, with a laugh.

Anita lives in Spain. She says
"Flamenco dancing's good!"
Olé! She shakes her tambourine!
I'd try it, if I could.

Coral's my Canadian chum.
When she can pitch her tent
Beside a little rocky stream,
She's happy and content.

Welsh Bronwen has a spinning-wheel.
It goes click-clack, click-clack!
She wears a shawl of cosy wool,
And hat, so tall and black.

Sometimes I think how I would love
To meet my pals, you know.
To shake their hands, and see them sm
And hear them say "Hello"!